Monkey and Elephant and a Secret Birthday Surprise

Monkey and Elephant and a Secret Birthday Surprise

shh

Carole Lexa Schaefer

illustrated by **Galia Bernstein**

CANDLEWICK PRESS

In celebration of Ivana, Becky, and Krisi,
Eva, William, and Sage
C. L. S.

For Alon
G. B.

Text copyright © 2015 by Carole Lexa Schaefer
Illustrations copyright © 2015 by Galia Bernstein

First paperback edition 2016

Library of Congress Catalog Card Number 2014945454
ISBN 978-0-7636-6131-1 (hardcover)
ISBN 978-0-7636-8744-1 (paperback)

16 17 18 19 20 TLF 10 9 8 7 6 5 4 3 2

Printed in Dongguan, Guangdong, China

This book was typeset in Triplex.
The illustrations were created digitally.

Candlewick Press
99 Dover Street
Somerville, Massachusetts 02144

visit us at www.candlewick.com

Contents

Chapter One
BEST FRIENDS

One morning, Monkey said,
"Elephant, you are my best friend.
I want to tell you a secret."

"Oh no, best friend. Please
don't," said Elephant.

"Why not?" said Monkey, scratching one pink ear.

"Because I already have a secret," said Elephant.

"Then let's share," said Monkey. "I will tell you my secret. And you tell me yours."

Elephant pushed his big ears against his cheeks, trying not to hear.

Monkey stood very close to him
and said, "I am getting older."
Elephant flapped his ears.
"That's not a secret," he said.

"No," said Monkey. "But today I am a whole year older."

"Ahh," said Elephant. "Today is your BIRTH—"

"Shh," said Monkey. "*That* is my secret."

"Why is that a secret?" asked Elephant, swishing his trunk.

"Because I do not like birthdays," said Monkey.

"Oh," said Elephant. "That's too bad."

"Now," said Monkey, "tell me your secret."

"Um," said Elephant.

Monkey patted his trunk. "It's okay, friend. I am good at keeping secrets."

"But I am not!" cried Elephant. "*That* is my secret."

"Yipes!" squealed Monkey.
"But, you *will* keep mine, won't
you? Tomorrow my birthday will
be over. You only have to keep my
secret for today."

"I will try, best friend," said
Elephant. He swayed from side
to side. "But, me oh my, I cannot
promise."

Chapter Two
NOT MY BIRTHDAY

Monkey was off picking berries.

Elephant thought, *How can I keep her secret safe while she is gone?*

He stepped inside their grass house. *Huh. I'll just hide in here.*

He closed everything tight—the
doors, the windows, even his eyes.
Just then, there was a knock on
the door. *Thump, thump, thump.*

"Hey ho, anyone home?" someone called.

"Uh-oh, company," said
Elephant. He opened the door.

"Good day, young Elephant,"
said Uncle Phump. "This is my
friend Clever Rat. He works at my
House for Making Hats."

"Howdy," said Clever.

"Hello," said Elephant. "I like
your cowboy hat."

"Clever can make any kind of hat," said Uncle Phump.

"I just made a new bunch of party hats," said Clever. "You must come and see them."

Party hats, thought Elephant. He flapped his ears. *Wup, wup, wup.*

"Yes," said Uncle Phump. "Come today."

"Today?" said Elephant.

Uncle Phump nodded. "No time like the present."

Presents, thought Elephant. He swished his tail. *Fwip, fwip, fwip.*

"I am not sure I can come today," said Elephant. "It is, um, someone's birthday."

"Oh, dear," said Uncle Phump. "Did I forget your birthday?"

"No," said Elephant. "Today is not *my* birthday."

"Well," said Uncle Phump, "it's not mine."

"It's not mine either," said Clever.

"Today is Monkey's birth—"
Elephant stopped. "I mean, could
Monkey come, too?"

"Of course," said Uncle Phump.

"We can make it a party," said Clever. "An It's-Not-My-Birthday party."

"That's clever, Clever," said Uncle Phump.

Elephant swayed from side to side. *Wump, wump.* "Um, how about making it a New-Hat party instead?"

"It can be both," said Uncle Phump. "Let's go get ready, Clever. See you later, Elephant."

"Whee-ew!" puffed Elephant. So far, he had kept Monkey's secret. But it was not easy. Who knew what might happen at an It's-Not-My-Birthday, New-Hat party?

Chapter Three
THE PARTY

"Look," said Monkey, "I picked more berries than we can eat."

"Let's take some to Uncle Phump," suggested Elephant.

"Great idea!" said Monkey. She turned a cartwheel.

Elephant tromped away with Monkey on his head.

Soon the two friends came to Uncle Phump's tall house.

"Come in. Come in," called Uncle
Phump.

"How pretty!" said Monkey,
looking around.

"The work of my friend Clever
Rat," said Uncle Phump.

"Howdy," said Clever.

"Nice work," said Monkey.

Just then, Cousin MeeMee and
her three babies tumbled in.

"My cousins!" squealed Monkey.
She hugged them all. "What are you
doing here?"

"Today is not my birthday," said Baby One.

"Not my birthday," said Baby Two.

"Not mine, hee-hee," said Baby Three, laughing.

33

"It's not my birthday either," said MeeMee. "But I brought a nice It's-Not-My-Birthday nut-crumble cake."

Monkey looked at Elephant.

"Yum!" said Elephant, flapping his ears.

"And here's some New-Hat coconut milk," said Uncle Phump. Monkey looked at Elephant.

"How sweet!" said Elephant, swishing his tail.

"And I made hats just for our It's-Not-My-Birthday, New-Hat party," said Clever.

Monkey looked at Elephant.

"What fun!" he said, swaying from side to side.

"Elephant," said Monkey, "what *is* an It's-Not-My-Birthday, New-Hat party?"

"Um, it's a party to celebrate today not being our birthdays, and to celebrate Clever's new hats," said Elephant.

"But," said Monkey, "today *is* my birth—"

"Monkey!" cried Elephant. "That is a secret!"

"What is a secret?" asked Mee-Mee, Uncle Phump, and Clever.

"What secret? What secret? What secret?" asked the babies.

"Today is my birthday," said Monkey.

"Why was that a secret?" asked Cousin MeeMee.

"Because Monkey does not like birthdays," said Elephant.

Monkey looked around the room. "Well," she said, "I think I might like *this* birthday."

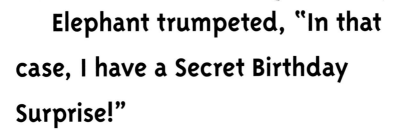

Elephant trumpeted, "In that case, I have a Secret Birthday Surprise!"

"What can it be?" asked Monkey.

Elephant brought out the nut cake—covered with birthday candles!

"Happy Birthday, Monkey!" said Elephant.

"And happy It's-Not-Your-Birthday, everyone else!" cheered Monkey. She blew out all the candles.

"Oh, yes. I like this birthday very, very much," she said. "And that is no secret."